D1354009

M and M

and the
Bad News Babies

by Pat Ross • pictures by Marylin Hafner

Fontana Young Lions

First published in the USA 1983
by Pantheon Books, a division of Random House, Inc.
First published in Great Britain
by Fontana Young Lions 1986
8 Grafton Street, London W1X 3LA

Fontana Young Lions is an imprint of
Fontana Paperbacks, a division of
the Collins Publishing Group

Printed in Great Britain
by William Collins Sons & Co. Ltd, Glasgow

Especially for
Richard and Benjamin
Kruger

CHAPTER ONE

Mandy put a pink sea castle
into the fish tank.
Mimi added six yellow stones
that glowed in the dark.
The friends M and M
had been fixing up the old fish tank
all week.
"Now all we need are the fish,"
said Mimi.
"But fish cost money,"
said Mandy.

Just then the doorbell rang.

"It's probably for your mother,"

said Mimi.

"My mother is downstairs

fixing her bike," said Mandy.

The doorbell kept ringing.

"We're coming!" shouted Mimi.

"Who's there?" said Mandy.

"It's your neighbour, Mrs Green,"

said the person in the hallway.

Mandy looked through the peephole

to make sure.

"It's Mrs Green all right."

Then there was a banging on the door.

"And guess who else," said Mandy.

"That's got to be Richie and Benjie,"
Mimi groaned.

"Don't open the door!"

"That would be rude," said Mandy.

"Okay, but I warned you," said Mimi.

"Those twins are bad news!"

Mandy opened the door part way.

The twins banged their bottles

against the door and smiled.

Richie always had

two bottles of milk.

Benjie always had

two bottles of juice.

That's how you could tell them apart.

"My mother is in the bike room,"

said Mandy, trying to be polite.

"Do you want to leave a message?"

"No thank you," said Mrs Green.

"I really wanted to leave the twins."

Mandy and Mimi looked very confused.

Then Mrs Green explained.

"I just have to dash to the store

for a few minutes."

Richie and Benjie

shoved the door wide open.

"Why, maybe you two could babysit,"
said Mrs Green.

"I won't be gone for long.

And your mother is just downstairs."

"We're working on a big project,"
said Mimi, thinking of the fish tank.

"I'd pay you," offered Mrs Green.

Mandy whispered to Mimi,

"We could buy *fish*!"

Mimi started to say no.

But Mandy quickly said,

"Okay Mrs Green, we'll do it!"

"You two are real babysitters now,"
said Mrs Green, smiling.

Richie and Benjie
left their bottles by the door
and crawled into the living room.
"What do we do?" asked Mandy.
"Oh, there's really nothing to it,"
said Mrs Green.
"Just make sure
they don't pick fuzz off the rug
and eat it.
Things like that.

If they play where they shouldn't
just say *no, no.*"
"That's what we say to my dog,"
said Mimi.
"Well, I'm sure the boys will be
good as gold," said Mrs Green.
"They have their bottles
and two wonderful babysitters,"
she added.
Then she waved goodbye.

CHAPTER TWO

Benjie started to dig in the dirt
around a big plant.
M and M remembered what to do.
"No, no," they said together.
"BOCK! BOCK!" shouted Benjie, happily.
"I bet he thinks it's a sandbox,"
groaned Mimi.

"No, no, Benjie. No sandbox."

Benjie shook his head and said,

"No, no, no, no!"

Then he licked the dirt

off his fingers.

Richie was busy playing with the TV.

He turned the sound up very loud.

Mandy ran over and turned off the TV.

"BOOM BOOM," said Richie.

"No boom boom," said Mandy.

"No, no, no, no!" said Richie.

And he started to cry.

Benjie started crying too.

"Now what do we do? shouted Mimi.

"We'll just have to play with them,"
said Mandy.

"That's what you do with babies."

"Yuck," said Mimi.

"I came here to play with you
and fix the fish tank.
I don't want to play
stupid baby games like peek-a-boo.
Think of something else
or I'm going home."

"Okay," Mandy shouted, "I've got it!
We can have a baby contest!"

Mimi made a face.

"If you mean a baby *beauty* contest,
they both lose," she said.

"No," said Mandy, "a baby *race* contest.
The first baby
across the living room wins.
One baby against the other."

"They'll never do it," said Mimi.

"It's worth a try," said Mandy.

"Okay, okay," said Mimi.

"But whatever we do,

we have to keep them away

from the fish tank."

So Mandy took Richie

and Mimi took Benjie.

"May the best baby win!" said Mandy.

Mandy and Mimi
quickly grabbed all four bottles.
Then they ran
to the other end of the room.
They held out the bottles
and shouted, "Go!"

Richie and Benjie
looked at their bottles.
Then they took off
crawling and rolling
and sliding and scooting.

Mandy shook Richie's bottles.

"Go baby, go!" she yelled.

"Milkie!" cried Richie.

Mimi shook Benjie's bottles.

"Juicie!" cried Benjie.

Richie and Benjie
reached their bottles
at the very same time.
It was a tie.

Mimi looked at the babies
sucking away.
"I just thought of a better contest,"
she said.
"It's a contest where *we* can beat
the babies!"

CHAPTER THREE

Mimi told Mandy about her contest—
a baby bottle sucking contest.
"It'll be us against the babies,"
said Mimi.
"May the best sucker win!"
said Mandy.

M and M put all four bottles
in a row.
"Let's fill them to the top,"
said Mimi.
"Two milks and two juices
coming up!"

The twins grabbed their bottles
and started the contest right away.
"Hurry," cried Mandy.
"One, two, three, GO!" shouted Mimi.
Then Mandy and Mimi began
to suck like babies, too.
But after a while Mimi cried, "Yuck!
The nipple's all wet and rubbery."

"It only *looks* easy,"

said Mandy.

"Look at Richie and Benjie.

They're sucking like machines!"

"We're just out of practice,"

said Mimi. "Keep going!"

So M and M did their best,

but they could not finish.

"I just bit my tongue," moaned Mandy.

"I just stopped!" cried Mimi.

"Let's see how the babies did."

On the floor near them

lay two empty bottles.

But no babies.

"They won all right," said Mimi.

"But where are they?" groaned Mandy.

"I bet they've eaten the plants,

chewed up my comic books,

wrecked my room and . . ."

"Wrecked the fish tank!"
screamed Mimi.

CHAPTER FOUR

Richie and Benjie were

by the fish tank.

"I think it's too late!" cried Mimi.

And she covered her eyes.

"What did they wreck?" cried Mandy,

looking for the terrible mess

she was sure they would find.

But all they saw were Richie and Benjie.

The babies were pointing
at the pink sea castle
and the six yellow stones.
Then they clapped.

"You can look now," Mandy told Mimi.

"I think they like it."

Mimi couldn't believe her eyes.

"What do you know," she said.

"I think those babies

are not such bad news after all."

M and M turned off the light
and showed the twins
how the six yellow stones
glowed in the dark.
"Oooo, oooo," said the twins.

Then M and M
told Richie and Benjie
about the new fish they would buy.
"Fishy, fishy, fishy,"
the twins said.

Before they knew it
Mrs Green was back.
"Ma! Ma!" Richie and Benjie yelled.
"Why, just look at your bottles!"
said Mrs Green.

"The twins were very thirsty,"
said Mandy.
Then Mrs Green
thanked Mimi and Mandy
and paid them each fifty pence.
Richie and Benjie banged their bottles
against the door on the way out.

"Now we can get fish!" said Mimi.
"One for each of us!" said Mandy.
Then they made silly fish faces
at each other.
Those silly fish faces
looked just like two babies
sucking on bottles.

And right away they knew
what they would name their fish.

"Richie," said Mandy.
"Benjie," said Mimi.
And nobody but the friends M and M
would ever know why.